Praise fo.

The Fix-It Friends: Have No Fear!

"Fears are scary! But don't worry: the Fix-It Friends know how to vanquish all kinds of fears, with humor and step-by-step help. Nicole C. Kear has written a funny and helpful series."

—**Fran Manushkin, author of the Katie Woo series**

"Full of heart and more than a little spunk, this book teaches kids that fear stands no chance against friendship and courage. Where were the Fix-It Friends when I was seven years old?"

—**Kathleen Lane, author of *The Best Worst Thing***

"I love the Fix-It Friends as a resource to give to the families I work with. The books help kids see their own power to overcome challenges—and they're just plain fun to read."

—**Lauren Knickerbocker, PhD, Co-Director, Early Childhood Service, NYU Child Study Center**

"Hooray for these young friends who work together; this diverse crew will have readers looking forward to more."

—*Kirkus Reviews*

The Fix-It Friends
Wish You Were Here

Nicole C. Kear
illustrated by Tracy Dockray

[Imprint]
MAKE YOUR MARK
NEW YORK

A part of Macmillan Publishing Group, LLC
175 Fifth Avenue, New York, NY 10010

THE FIX-IT FRIENDS: WISH YOU WERE HERE. Text copyright © 2017 by
Nicole C. Kear. Illustrations copyright © 2017 by Imprint. All rights
reserved. Printed in the United States of America by LSC Communications,
Harrisonburg, Virginia.

Library of Congress Cataloging-in-Publication Data

Names: Kear, Nicole C., author. | Dockray, Tracy, illustrator.
Title: The Fix-It Friends: wish you were here / Nicole C. Kear ; illustrations
by Tracy Dockray.
Other titles: Wish you were here
Description: First edition. | New York : Imprint, 2017. | Series: The Fix-It
Friends ; [4] | Summary: The Fix-It Friends are confronted with loss when
their friend's pet passes away. Includes a toolbox about grief and resources
for parents.
Identifiers: LCCN 2016056991 (print) | LCCN 2017027701 (ebook) |
ISBN 9781250086716 (Ebook) | ISBN 9781250086709 (pbk.) |
ISBN 9781250115799 (hardcover)
Subjects: | CYAC: Grief—Fiction. | Pets—Fiction. | Helpfulness—Fiction. |
Brothers and sisters—Fiction. | Friendship—Fiction. | Schools—Fiction.
Classification: LCC PZ7.1.K394 (ebook) | LCC PZ7.1.K394 Fkm 2017 (print) |
DDC [Fic]—dc23
LC record available at https://lccn.loc.gov/2016056991

Our books may be purchased in bulk for promotional, educational, or
business use. Please contact your local bookseller or the Macmillan
Corporate and Premium Sales Department at (800) 221-7945 ext. 5442 or by
e-mail at MacmillanSpecialMarkets@macmillan.com.

Book design by Ellen Duda
Illustrations by Tracy Dockray
Imprint logo designed by Amanda Spielman

First edition, 2017

ISBN 978-1-250-11579-9 (hardcover)

1 3 5 7 9 10 8 6 4 2

ISBN 978-1-250-08670-9 (paperback)

1 3 5 7 9 10 8 6 4 2

ISBN 978-1-250-08671-6 (ebook)

mackids.com

If you steal this book, get ready for a hammerhead shark to eat you
for dinner, because that's what will happen.
Trust me. My name is Little Nicky and I know stuff.

For David, who gets me through the muck

With special thanks to expert consultant
Rebecca Rialon Berry, PhD, of the NYU Child Study Center

Chapter 1

My name is Veronica Conti, and what I want, more than anything in the world, is a pet.

"You already have a pet!" my mom always says.

"Mom, you know I love Fred," I reply. "But I want a pet you can snuggle! And you can*not* snuggle a goldfish."

I found that out the hard way when I was three years old and I tried to cuddle our very first goldfish, Swimmy. I climbed on top of my dresser to reach the tank. Then I stuck my hand in the cold water. I was juuuuuust about to scoop Swimmy up so I could give him a big smooch. But before

I could, my big brother, Jude, walked in and screamed his head off.

Right away, Mom and Dad moved the fish tank into their bedroom and put a big, heavy cover on it. With a lock!

So if there is one thing I know, it is that you cannot cuddle, or snuggle, or smooch a goldfish.

You can't even pet one, for crying out loud. I want a pet you can pet!

So for Christmas every year, I ask my parents for one. I asked this year, too:

Veronica Laverne Conti's ☆ Christmas List ☆

1. A dog who I will name Spork.
2. A cat who I will name Lady Godiva.
3. A guinea pig who I will name Rodeo.
4. A hamster who I will name Dirty Harry.
5. A rabbit who I will name Houdini.
6. A chinchilla who I will name Mr. Roosevelt (Turn over)

Christmas List continued

7. A hot glue gun.
8. A microphone.
9. A curly red wig.
10. 100 business cards. They should say:
Dr. Veronica Laverne Conti
President
The Fix-It Friends
718-555-3217

I wanted these business cards so that if I met a kid with a problem on the playground or the subway or in a helicopter, I could hand the kid my card and say, "My associates and I can help. Call me." How cool would *that* be?

I got almost everything on my Christmas list, except for the business cards. Mom said I wasn't allowed to give out our phone number. Jude said I wasn't the president of the Fix-It Friends, because all the members of our group—me, Jude, Cora, and Ezra—are equal. He also told me I was not a doctor.

That is true, but it does make me sound more professional.

But it doesn't matter anyway, because I didn't get any business cards for Christmas. Oh, and you know what else I didn't get?

A pet!

Chapter 2

After we opened all our presents on Christmas morning, Dad went into the kitchen to make chocolate-chip pancakes. My little sister, Pearl, went to help. She is only two years old, so her idea of helping is to eat half of the chocolate chips while Dad is making the batter.

Jude and I helped Mom clean up all the wrapping paper. I like to smash the used-up paper into balls and toss them in a garbage bag, yelling, "SCORE!"

Jude likes to find big pieces of wrapping paper

that are not torn too badly. Then he folds them nice and neat, to use for next year.

Guess who gets done faster? This girl.

While we were cleaning, I asked my mom why I didn't get any of the pets on my Christmas list.

"You know your father's allergic to anything with fur," Mom said with a sigh.

"Well, I'm allergic to Jude, and I still have to live with him," I replied.

Jude scowled at me.

"I'm just kidding," I said, even though I sort of wasn't.

Mom tied the top of the big garbage bag. I stuck on the red curly wig I got for Christmas.

I asked for it because my best friend, Cora, who is in the second grade just like me, has red curly hair. She gets everything her heart desires. I think these two things are related. Grown-ups cannot resist her cuteness. So I wanted to see if the magic hair would work for me, too.

"Oh, Mommy Dear," I said. I always call my mom "Mom" except for when I want something, and then I call her Mommy Dear. "What about a little, teeny, tiny guinea pig? Like Ezra has?"

Mom laughed when she saw me in the wig.

"Nice try," she said.

"I don't know why they're called guinea pigs," I said. "What is a guinea, anyway?"

"It's an old kind of money. Also a place in Africa," said Jude. He is in fourth grade, so he thinks he knows absolutely everything.

I just ignored him and kept talking: "And they don't look anything like pigs! I mean, Ziggy's about a million times cuter than a pig, with his long brown fur. He doesn't sound anything like a pig, either. He doesn't snort; he squeaks. Every time he sees me, he starts squeaking like crazy. It's exactly like he is saying, 'Hi! Let's play!' "

"Ziggy is so smart," agreed Jude. "If you say his name, he runs right over to you."

"Maybe we can visit Ezra and Ziggy this afternoon," I said hopefully.

"We can't," replied Mr. Party Pooper. "Ezra went to Jamaica for Christmas, to see his grandparents."

Jude always knows exactly where Ezra is because they've been best friends since first grade.

"And Cora went to Long Island to visit *her* grandparents for Hanukkah! So half of the Fix-It Friends are gone! We can't even have a meeting. How boring can you get?"

I flopped down on the couch and yanked on my wig curls to make them *boing*! "I wish Nana and Nonno had taken me with them to Italy."

I really want to go to Italy because my nonno said they have the best ice cream there and you *always* get free whipped cream on top. Plus, I would like to see if the Leaning Tower of Pisa really does lean over like that. I can't speak Italian, but I can speak English with an Italian accent, which

I learned by copying my grandma—you-a just-a talk-a like-a this-a! So I begged Nana and Nonno to take me with them. But they said they were going for a whole month and I'd miss too much school. "Even better," I said. They just laughed, even though I was not kidding.

"None of my friends are here," I grumbled to Mom. "Everyone went somewhere else!"

"Speaking of going places," said Mom, sitting down next to me on the couch. "Dad and I are taking a little trip, starting on New Year's Day. I have to go to a conference in California, so we're turning the trip into a romantic getaway."

"Ewwww, gross," Jude and I said at the same time.

Then Jude added, "But who's going to watch us?"

"Well, that's the exciting part!" said Mom

with a big smile. "We're having some special guests!"

Jude and I looked at each other and smiled. We knew just who the special guests would be.

"Granny and Gramps! Granny and Gramps! Granny and Gramps!" Jude and I chanted together.

Granny and Gramps are my mom's parents. They live in Texas, which is where my mom is from. Whenever they visit, they spoil us rotten.

"Yep," said Mom. "They're staying for a whole week and a half! And they're bringing another special guest with them."

"Aunt Alice!!!" I shrieked.

Aunt Alice is Mom's kid sister and my favorite aunt. She makes her own dresses and has three tattoos and knows how to belly dance. Mom calls her a "free spirit." She lives in Texas, too.

"Well, no," Mom replied. "Aunt Alice is going to a yoga-teacher-training retreat, so she can't make it."

"Bummer," said Jude. "But at least that means Little Nicky isn't coming."

Little Nicky is Aunt Alice's son. He is four years old and he is—how can I put this nicely?—a hideous nightmare.

Here's a list of Little Nicky's favorite activities:

1. Talking about hammerhead sharks. Except he never just talks like a regular person. HE SHOUTS EVERYTHING HE SAYS.

2. Singing songs about hammerhead sharks.

3. Pretending to be a hammerhead shark.

4. Saying that everything, except for hammerhead sharks, is stupid.

5. Destroying people's prized possessions.

Jude and I both love Aunt Alice, but we can't stand Little Nicky.

"I'm so glad Little Nicky isn't coming!" I exclaimed.

"Well, actually . . . ," said Mom, biting her lip.

"Mommy Dear," I said, trying to stay calm. "Please, *please* don't tell me Little Nicky's coming."

"Well, yes, he has to," replied Mom, "because Granny and Gramps are babysitting him while Aunt Alice goes to the yoga retreat."

"Why can't his dad watch him?" I moaned.

"Uncle Eddy's deployed," said Mom. "He won't be home for a few months."

The Fix-It Friends

Uncle Eddy is a sailor in the navy. When he's deployed, he sails away to far-off places on a humongous ship for months. Sometimes he can't even tell us where he's going, because it's top secret.

"So Little Nicky has to come," Mom explained.

"Noooooooooo!" I howled. Then I rolled off the couch and lay totally still on the carpet as if I'd died from the horror of it.

"Veronica Laverne." My mom frowned. "He's only four years old. Have some patience."

I revived myself so I could reply, "How can I have patience with someone who eats all the candy out of my favorite Pez dispensers and squirts hand soap in my hairbrush and scribbles in my diary?"

"Remember when he took my copy of *Attack of the Santa Clones* and tore the front cover off? On purpose?" Jude exclaimed. "That was a very rare book! It was a collector's item!"

Mom rubbed her forehead like she had a headache.

"And that's nothing compared to what he did to Pearl!" Jude pointed out.

"Do you mean when he hid her Christmas stocking under the sink so we didn't find it until after Easter? Or when he threw all her pacis in the toilet bowl? Or do you mean when he cut off a big chunk of her hair?"

Mom stood up.

"Your dad and I will only be gone about a week," she said. "I think you can survive. And I expect you to be good hosts. He is your cousin, after all."

Chapter 3

Granny, Gramps, and Little Nicky arrived on New Year's Day. Mom and Dad let us stay up till twelve o'clock the night before to watch the ball drop on TV. So I was still sleeping in my bed, which is the bottom bunk, when they came. I was having the most wonderful dream.

I was wearing a red shiny leotard like an Olympic gymnast, and I was doing perfect back handsprings through a field of white daisies. The daisies were so bright and pretty that I popped one in my mouth. It melted instantly into whipped cream! Then as I was stuffing the flowers in my mouth as fast as I could, an adorable bulldog ran up and wagged her tail. She said, "My name is Pancake and I am your very own dog." And then a whole bunch of baby bulldogs popped out of her ears, and they said, "We're your dogs, too! Pet us! Pet us!" I was scratching their bellies and feeding them daisies, and then, all of a sudden, the puppies shouted in a terrible voice, "DO YOU HAVE ANY TUNA FISH?"

But it wasn't the puppies shouting. It was Little Nicky. He was standing right next to my bed.

This is what Little Nicky looks like:

1. Very short. He's as tall as Pearl, even though he's two years older than her.

2. Dark blond hair that is shaved on the sides and spiky in a strip up top. This hairstyle is called a Mohawk. Little Nicky thinks it makes his hair look like a shark fin.

3. Ears that stick out.

4. A big mouth, which is always open because he is always talking.

"I'M STARVING AND GRANNY WANTS ME TO EAT CEREAL. BUT I TOLD HER CEREAL IS STUPID. HAMMERHEAD SHARKS NEVER EAT CEREAL. THEY EAT TUNA FISH."

I heard Jude groan loudly in the top bunk.

I looked at the clock on my desk. It was only 8:31 a.m.

"Little Nicky," I croaked. "When did you get here?"

"WE GOT ON THE PLANE SO EARLY THAT IT WAS STILL DARK OUTSIDE," he shouted. "IT WENT REALLY FAST BUT NOT AS FAST AS A HAMMERHEAD SHARK. WHY IS IT SO COLD IN THIS PLACE? I HATE COLD STUFF."

I put my pillow over my head. I had just woken up, and I *already* had a headache.

That night, after dinner, it was time for Mom and Dad to leave for California. When they tried to zip up their suitcase, they found Pearl curled up inside it. She was sucking away on Chooch, her favorite pacifier.

She popped Chooch out of her mouth and said, "I'm wittle! Take me!"

Wish You Were Here

"Oh, Pearl, my girl," said Dad, lifting her up, "we'll be home in a week. And you'll have so much fun with Gramps and Granny."

He did not say anything about Little Nicky. He's no dummy.

Mom kissed Pearl on the top of her head. "And you'll have Jude and Ronny."

"You mean Veronica," I corrected her.

"You'll have Jude and Veronica by your side," said Mom. "And Ricardo!"

Ricardo is a stuffed rat. He is also the love of Pearl's life. He has dirty black fur, no whiskers, and a tail that's stuck on with silver duct tape.

Pearl is always worried that someone is going to steal Ricardo. This is really funny because Ricardo's so old and broken-down, the only person who might take him is the garbageman.

Mom pulled Ricardo out of the suitcase, where Pearl had stuffed him.

"Yikes! We almost took him with us," said Mom, smiling. "Imagine how much you'd have missed him!"

Then she handed Ricardo to Pearl, said good-bye, and walked out the door with Dad.

Chapter 4

The next morning, I had to go back to school. Usually, I hate the end of winter break.

Homework? Blegh.

Spelling tests? Ewww.

Math? Have mercy!

But this time, I was glad to be going back to school. Spending a whole day with Little Nicky is even worse than a double-sided sheet of double-digit subtraction problems. Plus I couldn't wait to give out the holiday presents I got for my friends!

For Cora, I had a travel sewing kit that I got from a hotel. It had five colors of thread, a needle,

and two buttons inside. It did not have any sequins, which is probably for the best. When Cora made costumes for the school play, she went bananas with sequins.

For both Noah and Cora's twin sister, Camille, I had key chains. Noah's had a little soccer ball attached to it, and Camille's had a basketball. I got them as prizes from the dentist's office. Usually you get to choose only one or two prizes, but I sweet-talked the dentist into letting me take

four. Sweet-talking is one of my specialties.

For Minnie, I had a pretty pink plastic headband with a black bow on it. Nana gave it to me for Christmas before she left for Italy. I guess Nana for-

got that I hate headbands. They
make me feel like my head's getting pinched by a gigantic crab.
But I knew Minnie would love it.

For Ezra, I had a very special present: an adorable vest for Ziggy! I made it with my own two
hands and my new hot-glue gun. I didn't know
Ziggy's size, so I used Velcro to make the vest ad-

justable. I cut it out of green felt,
and then I glued a red *Z* on the
back. I couldn't wait for Ziggy
to try it on!

I gave out almost all the presents at recess.
I felt like Santa Claus!

The only person I couldn't find was Ezra. So
I looked for Jude, because Ezra is almost always
with him.

I spotted Jude sitting next to the Lost and

Found bin, with a pad of paper and a pen on his lap.

"Did you lose something?" I asked him.

"Me? Don't be preposterous!" he snorted. His glasses had slid down his nose, so he pushed them back up with his finger. "I'm on recess mediator duty, but no one needs me. So I thought I'd make a list of the items in the Lost and Found and tape it on the outside."

"But people can just look inside the bin," I pointed out.

"Yes, but this is much more *organized*," he explained.

I don't know why I bothered to argue with him. When Jude starts making a list, there is no stopping him. Over the winter break, he made a list of all the lists he wanted to write. I am not even kidding. I found it on his desk:

<u>List of Lists to Write</u>
1. List of New Year's Resolutions
2. List of Books to Read
3. List of Movies to make with Ezra
4. List of My Stuff that Ronny Has Lost or Stolen
5. List of Consequences for Ronny Losing or Stealing My Stuff
6. List of Reasons I Should Get My Own Room

So I didn't try to stop Jude from making a dumb Lost and Found list that nobody needed.

Instead, I asked him, "Have you seen Ezra?"

Jude frowned. "Something's wrong with Ezra. He's in his mom's office."

"There's nothing weird about that," I replied. Ezra's mom is the principal of our school, and he goes to her office all the time—to ask her a question or because he forgot something, stuff like that.

"I know," said Jude, "but he's acting really weird. He hardly said a word to me all morning."

"Have no fear!" I exclaimed. "I will get to the bottom of this!"

Before Jude could reply, I ran straight to the red double doors that lead to the school—and to the principal's office.

Chapter 5

You have to walk into the main office to get to Principal Powell's office. When I got there, her door was closed, which means "Do Not Disturb." I decided to hang around and try to hear what Ezra and his mom were talking about.

The ladies who work in the main office, especially the principal's secretary, do not like kids hanging around there. You have to seem like you are there for a very good reason or they tell you to scram.

Principal Powell's secretary was not sitting at her desk, which made it a little easier to wait. I acted

like I was looking at the stacks of brochures over there, but really, I was trying to eavesdrop. I am pretty good at this because I do it all the time in front of the door to my mom's office. Her office is on the bottom floor of our house, so I can't help it if I just end up down there sometimes.

It is pretty hard to hear what my mom's clients are saying because she has a lot of machines plugged into the wall, which all make noise. She does it on purpose so her clients can tell her all their secrets without anyone overhearing. My mom is a therapist, which means she listens to people talk about their troubles and then she tries to make them feel better. I asked her if she tells a lot of jokes, and she said no, so who the heck knows what she does? All I know is, when I listen at the door to her office, I hardly ever hear anything.

It was way easier to eavesdrop on Principal Powell and Ezra. I heard the crying right away.

I thought maybe Ezra was crying because he got his braces tightened and they hurt. Maybe Gary Grotowski said something mean to him. Maybe he was crying because he missed his dad, who lives in another state.

While I was busy wondering, Principal Powell's grumpy secretary came back to her desk.

Her name is Rose Mackenzie . . . or it might be

Mackenzie Rose. I can never remember. Both her names sound like first names!

So just to be safe, I call her "ma'am." I can tell she thinks I'm playing some kind of joke on her, but I'm not. Because of this, she is very suspicious of me. Also I think she is still mad at me for knocking over the PENNIES FOR THE RAIN FOREST can in the office and for causing a fiasco with a fake spider.

Mrs. Rose or Mackenzie is very old. She looks much older than Miss Tibbs and all my grandparents. I am dying to ask her how old she is, but my mom says I'm not allowed to. I am guessing that she's 104.

Her hair is completely white and it is always pulled into a tiny little bun near her neck. She wears red rectangular glasses pushed aaaaaall the way down to the end of her nose.

Wish You Were Here

She is like the guard of Principal Powell's office because her desk is right by the door. Nobody can go in or come out of that office without her seeing.

"Veronica," said Mrs. Rose or Mackenzie. "Don't you have somewhere to be?"

"Who, me?" I asked. "I'm just reading this brochure about—"

I grabbed the brochure that was closest to my hand and read it out loud.

"Wart removal," I said.

"Having a problem with warts, are you?" Mrs. Rose or Mackenzie asked. Her eyebrows were raised so high, they practically hit the ceiling.

"Oh, I've got loads of warts. I'm covered in 'em. I've got a humongous hairy one right on my belly button."

Just then, the door to Principal Powell's office opened. Ezra shuffled out, blowing his nose into a tissue, with his mom behind him.

"Ez!" I chirped. "Hi! Happy New Year!"

"Hi," he mumbled, looking down. He seemed so sad. I just really, really, really wanted to cheer him up.

"Hey, I have something special for you!" I exclaimed, handing him the present I had put in my pocket. "Actually, it's for Ziggy. He is going to love it!"

Wish You Were Here

All of a sudden, Ezra's mouth twisted to the side and he made a choking noise in his throat.

Then Ezra spoke. But it didn't sound like Ezra at all. First of all, he wasn't talking in his usual super-speedy way. He was talking slowly, with pauses in between his words.

Second of all, he was being really mean! And Ezra is never mean to me.

"I don't . . . want . . . your dumb . . . present!" he growled. "Ziggy WON'T love it! Ziggy won't love ANYTHING!"

To my horror, he threw the present right on the dirty floor and ran out.

I was so surprised, I could not even gasp. I just stared down at the gift and started to feel really sad. I felt a big lump in my throat like I'd just swallowed a golf ball. I gulped hard, and then I asked Principal Powell, "What's he talking about?"

"Why don't you come in, my dear?" she said. "We'll talk."

I picked up the present for Ziggy and walked past Principal Powell into her office.

Chapter 6

I know a principal's office is supposed to be a terrible place that makes your teeth chatter in fear, but actually, Principal Powell's office is cozy and wonderful. It has a red couch that is super comfy and soft. When you sit in it, you feel like you are sinking into a strawberry cloud. There is a table in front of the couch, which always has crayons and construction paper and scratch 'n' sniff stickers on it. Fancy music with violins is always playing in the background.

Plus Principal Powell has cool posters on her wall with cheerful sayings like, "The mind is like a parachute. It works best when open" and "The best dreams happen when you are awake."

"Would you like some tea?" she asked, holding up a silver thermos. I nodded.

Every time I go to Ezra's house, I have the same hibiscus tea. In the summer, it's iced, and in the winter, it's hot. Principal Powell always puts lots of honey in it so it's sweet, and it smells wonderful. That's because it's made of real flowers!

Principal Powell poured the tea into two mugs and handed one to me. Then she took a long sip and said, "I have to apologize for Ezra's behavior. I don't want you to take it personally."

Principal Powell has a way of talking that makes it sound like she is singing. I think it's because she lived in Jamaica until she was a teenager. I love the way she talks.

Wish You Were Here

I took a nice, big sip of the tea, which made me feel warm from the inside out.

"What did Ezra mean about Ziggy?" I asked.

"I'm so sorry to tell you this," said Principal Powell, "but Ziggy has died."

I shook my head. That was impossible!

"But—but—but—" My mind was racing around. I couldn't even think straight. "But I just saw Ziggy! Right before Christmas, when we came over to make cookies at your house! He was squeaking like always! He was fine!"

"That is true," agreed Principal Powell, "but you know, we've had Ziggy for many years. He was very, very old for a guinea pig."

"Did he die while you were gone? Maybe the person who was babysitting him did something wrong. Did you call the police?"

"He was in wonderful hands while we were gone, with my neighbor," Principal Powell said. "And, in any event, it happened the day after we came back from vacation. It was nobody's fault. Ziggy was just very old."

I felt like my arms and legs weighed about 500 pounds, like I couldn't move even if you offered me a triple-scoop ice cream sundae with extra whipped cream.

Then the big lump in my throat came back, but it wasn't the size of a golf ball anymore. It was the size of a soccer ball. Some tears started to slide down my cheeks, and Principal Powell passed me a tissue box.

"Yes, it's hard. I'm sad about it, too," she said. "Ziggy was a member of our family."

We were both quiet for a minute. Then Principal Powell spoke again: "Will you tell Jude the

news? I don't want him to think Ezra's mad at him."

I nodded and looked down. I was still holding the present for Ziggy. That present made me feel so sad, I had to stay in the office for the rest of recess. When I left, I tossed the present right in the trash.

Chapter 7

That afternoon, Gramps picked up Jude and me from school. I told them the terrible news about Ziggy.

"It's tough when you lose a pet," said Gramps. "Y'all remember my black Lab Tucker? He died 'bout five years back. I still miss that dog. Used to bring me my slippers when I came home in the evening. It 'bout near broke my heart to see those slippers after he died."

"Poor Ezra. He probably feels miserable every time he goes home and sees Ziggy's empty cage," said Jude.

"You should invite him to our house tomorrow," I suggested. "Cora could come over, too, and we can have a Fix-It meeting! We can think of ways to help Ez!"

Jude nodded.

But at pickup the next day, Jude said Ezra didn't want to have a meeting. He didn't want to talk about Ziggy. In fact, he didn't feel like coming over at all. He said he just wanted to be left alone.

Since Cora was coming over anyway, we decided to have a Fix-It meeting about Ezra, without Ezra.

As soon as we got home, we grabbed leftover candy canes and went into the bedroom Jude and I share, where we hoped Little Nicky would leave us alone.

"Guys, this is serious! I've never seen Ezra so upset," I said. "What can we do to help?"

"We could leave him alone, like he told us to," Jude said.

"Have you no heart?" I cried. "Leave him alone in his time of need!"

"It's what he wants!" Jude replied.

"Well, *I* want a black poodle named Lexington to sleep in my bed with me, and I'm not getting that!" I said. "So we can't always get what we want!"

"That doesn't make one iota of sense," said Jude. "Not even one iota."

"Well, one thing is for sure," said Cora, who is always good at breaking up fights. "We definitely can't mention Ziggy or guinea pigs or pets or anything like that for a while."

"Absolutely," I agreed. "And we should be extra nice to him. And we should do all his favorite stuff, to cheer him up."

"I *could* ask if he wants to finish filming *Shimmy Strikes Back*," Jude agreed. "He's been wanting to do that for a while."

One of Jude and Ezra's favorite things to do is make funny horror movies, like *Shimmy Strikes Back*. It's about a crazed squirrel named Shimmy who goes on a rampage until Chiller the killer pigeon fights back. I am terrific at doing different accents, so they asked me to do the voice of Shimmy. I gave him an English accent like my drama teacher, Ginger Frost. It cracks us all up.

"*Now* you're talking, Jude!" I exclaimed.

"HEY!" boomed Little Nicky's voice in my ear. He had crept in and was sitting next to us, like he was a Fix-It Friend. Outrageous!

"ARE THERE ANY SHARKS IN THIS MOVIE?" asked Little Nicky. "GREAT WHITES? MAKOS? SAND TIGERS? HAMMERHEADS?"

"Ummm, no," said Jude.

"THEN IT'S STUPID," Little Nicky announced. He stood up, stuck out his tongue, and took a big, slobbery lick of Cora's candy cane. Then he walked right out of the room, like he couldn't waste his time on such nonsense.

"I don't think I want this anymore," said Cora, tossing her candy cane in the trash.

Jude called Ezra to see if he wanted to film *Shimmy Strikes Back* that weekend. Ezra said he didn't feel like it yet, but maybe on Monday.

To make matters worse, it was freezing cold all weekend, so we were stuck inside the apartment with Little Nicky the whole time. He spent half of every day in the tub, playing with his plastic shark collection. He stayed in the water so long, his fingers got all wrinkly and he looked like a swamp creature.

One time, I went in the bathroom, closed the door, and was about to sit on the toilet. All of a sudden, I heard an enormous ruckus from the bathtub. Who should pull back the shower curtain but Little Nicky? He was hiding in there and I had no idea! I screamed so loud that he dived back under the water.

Little Nicky was supposed to sleep on an air mattress in Mom and Dad's room, but after just two nights, he refused.

"THIS AIR BED IS FREEZING AND STUPID AND IT GIVES ME A HEADACHE SO I CAN'T SLEEP A WINK!" he complained. "I WANNA SLEEP IN PEARL'S BED!"

Then he threw such a big, screaming fit that Pearl said he could sleep in her bed and she'd sleep on the air mattress. But, of course, the only room she wanted to sleep in was mine. So, because of

Wish You Were Here

Little Nicky, I had to share a room with *both* my siblings!

I couldn't wait for Little Nicky to hit the road. I couldn't even wait for the weekend to be over. I have never been so excited to go back to school on Monday morning.

Chapter 8

After school on Monday, Granny came to pick us up with Pearl. Thankfully, Little Nicky had stayed at home with Gramps.

Pearl was in her stroller, tucked under a blue fleece blanket, wearing a white hat with mouse ears and whiskers on it. She looked adorable. She also looked miserable.

Her lower lip stuck out really far, and it was trembling. Dad calls this the Pearl Power Pout.

"Pearly Pie!" I exclaimed. "What's the matter?"

"Wicawdo," she moaned. "Wicawdo's gone."

Wish You Were Here

My heart dropped like a heavy stone, right down into my stomach.

Since her second birthday, when Pearl got Ricardo, she has never spent a night without him. One time, over the summer, Pearl left Ricardo at the Monroe, which is the building where Dad works as a super. She didn't realize he was gone until it was time to go to sleep. Then she cried and cried until Dad finally walked over to the Monroe in his pj's and brought Ricardo home.

Now, whenever we go anywhere, Mom and Dad always look at the checklist hanging by our front door. Jude made it, of course.

It says:

1. Wallet?
2. Phone?
3. Keys?
4. Ricardo?

Of all those things, Ricardo is the most important.

"Don't worry, Pearly," I told her. "We'll find him."

While I was busy talking to Pearl, Jude walked over. And guess who was with him?

"EZRA!" I hollered as I threw my arms around him. Then I let go and looked at him to make sure he was okay. He wasn't dancing a jig or jumping for joy, but he was not crying and his eyes didn't look red.

Wish You Were Here

"I'm so glad to see you!" I exclaimed. "You have to tell us alllll about Jamaica! Did you catch any lizards? What did you get for Christmas? Did you eat any jerk chickens?"

In Jamaica, there is a kind of food called jerk chicken. But people don't call it that because the chicken did something rude and they're mad at it. "Jerk" is the name of the spices they put on it. I ate it at Ezra's house one time, and it was so delicious, I had three helpings. Then I cracked everyone up by saying, "This chicken may be a jerk, but he sure is tasty!"

"Yeah, we had jerk chicken and also pepper pot soup with pigs' tails in it—"

"Real tails?" I cried.

"Yeah, real ones, cut into pieces, and— Oh! Jude, listen to this! My grandfather taught me how to drain a coconut and get the milk out. It's so cool! You jam a screwdriver into this little soft spot. . . ."

I sighed with relief. Ezra was talking a mile a minute, so fast you could hardly understand a word he was saying. Good old Ezra was back.

As soon as we got home, Pearl ran right into her bedroom to look for Ricardo. Little Nicky was watching a TV show about fish in the living room. Jude and Ezra headed into the kitchen to make their signature nacho dish, called the Fire-Breathing Dragon. It's called that because they put Tabasco on top. It's too spicy for me, but I didn't complain, because I was trying to keep Ezra happy.

After Jude and Ezra stuffed themselves silly, Jude got all the things for the movie—his camera, the *Shimmy Strikes Back* script, and Shimmy, who is a very cuddly stuffed animal. We went into our bedroom to start filming, and Jude handed me Shimmy, the cute, brown, adorable furball. All of a sudden, I gasped.

Cute!

Brown!

Adorable!

Furball!

I'd never thought of it before, but Shimmy looked so much like Ziggy! Too much! A warning siren went off in my head.

I said, "Umm, guys, you know what? I don't feel like making the movie after all."

Ezra and Jude both looked totally confused.

"What's up?" asked Ezra.

"Nothing," I said, shrugging. "I just don't feel like it."

"But we're at the most important part!" Jude

exclaimed. "We need you to do Shimmy's voice. You're the only one who can do the accent."

"It's just not a good idea," I said to Jude. I opened my eyes very wide to get my point across. "Just DROP it!"

"What do you mean?" asked Jude. Sometimes he can be *so* thickheaded. "Why, huh? Why?"

"BECAUSE YOU'LL MAKE EZRA THINK ABOUT HOW ZIGGY'S DEAD!" I shouted. I really didn't mean to shout. I just got so fed up with Jude and his thick head.

Wish You Were Here

Ezra's face crumpled up all of a sudden.

"Excuse me," he said as he bolted to the bathroom.

"Ronny!" Jude cried. "Look what you *did*! What's the *matter* with you?"

"It's *your* fault! We said we weren't going to talk about anything that would make Ezra think about Ziggy!"

"But he *wasn't* thinking about Ziggy until you made a huge deal about it and reminded him!"

"But I was just trying to help!"

"Every time you try to help, you make things worse!" he hollered. "Just leave us alone!"

At that moment, Pearl ran into our bedroom and flopped down on the floor.

"Wicawdooooooooo!!" she sobbed. "I need you!"

"I'm going to check on Ez," said Jude, and he stormed off.

I knelt down next to Pearl. She looked at me, with her big blue eyes all watery.

"When did you see Ricardo last? And where?"

"This mowning, in my woom!" Pearl sniffled.

"Well, he's got to be there, then, because nobody's been in your room today. Jude and I have been at school, and who else—"

All of a sudden, I remembered someone else who had been in Pearl's room that day. Someone whose favorite activity was destroying people's prized possessions.

"Little Nicky!" I yelped.

"Wittle Nicky!" Pearl growled. She balled her fists up and squeezed tight.

Pearl and I tiptoed into Mom and Dad's bedroom, which was where Little Nicky's backpack was. We searched through the whole thing, but we couldn't find Ricardo anywhere. We were just starting to put all his sharks and books and stuff back in the backpack when Gramps walked in with Little Nicky right behind him.

"HEY!" he shouted. "WHY ARE YOU TOUCHING MY STUFF?"

Pearl made a low growling noise. Her top lip was curled up in a sneer so you could see her teeth. She looked like a dog ready to attack.

"Gimme Wicawdo!" she yelled.

"WHO'S WICAWDO?" Little Nicky asked.

"Ricardo is Pearl's stuffed rat and you know it," I said.

"WHY WOULD I TOUCH A RAT?" replied Little Nicky. "RATS ARE STUPID!"

"Wicawdo's NOT stupid!" The words exploded

out of Pearl. Then she leaped up and pushed Little
Nicky down with all her might.

"Pearl!" Gramps scolded, pulling her off Little
Nicky. "What's the matter?"

"Ricardo's missing, and the only person who's
been in Pearl's room all day was Little Nicky," I explained. Then I turned to Little Nicky and said,
"You have to give Ricardo back to her! She needs
him! It's not a funny joke!"

"BUT I DON'T HAVE HIM!" Little Nicky's
face was getting all red.

"Now, let's just hold our horses for a second,"

Gramps said. He never raises his voice, but you can tell when he means business. "I reckon that's enough slinging around accusations without any proof. Most likely, Pearl just put the critter down somewhere and forgot about it. Let's hunker down and look for him."

So we did. I searched the living room, where Ezra and Jude were sitting on the couch, doing homework. They were not talking at all.

Ezra's eyes looked red, and his face was shiny from crying. I felt terrible about what I'd done. I wanted to apologize, but I figured I should probably leave them alone. So after I searched the living room for Ricardo, I just went into my bedroom and did my homework, too. I even did the double-sided math sheet. When I came out, Ezra had gone home.

Guess who found Ricardo?

No one.

And guess who couldn't go to sleep that night? Everyone!

Pearl lay on the air mattress in our room and asked for Ricardo over and over again. Then she started asking for Mom and Dad.

Granny read Pearl about twenty books, and then Gramps sang her about thirty verses of the song "Froggy Went A-Courting." They gave her three pacis—one to suck on and one to hold in each hand. But she was just too sad to sleep. So finally, way after her bedtime—way after my bedtime, even—Granny and Gramps let her sleep in bed with them.

I thought that finding Ricardo might be a good job for the Fix-It Friends—but then I thought that if Shimmy had reminded Ezra of Ziggy, Ricardo would probably do the same thing. If I wanted to ever get any sleep, I'd just have to find Ricardo myself.

Chapter 9

The next day at lunch, I almost fell asleep while I was eating the pimiento cheese sandwich Granny had packed for me.

I heard a voice next to me ask, "Miss Conti, are you ill?"

I knew who it was before I opened my eyes. Only one person calls me Miss Conti.

Standing before me was Miss Tibbs, the most dreaded recess and lunch teacher on the planet. Miss Tibbs's beady black eyes were staring at me from behind her big black glasses. She is super strict, and she always has her eye on me.

Her voice was like a bucket of cold water in my face. It woke me right up!

"I'm not sick," I replied. "I'm tust jired, I mean, just tired."

Miss Tibbs made a *harrumph* sound, which is her favorite sound to make.

"A good night's rest is essential to your health," she lectured me. "I, myself, am always in bed by eight p.m. sharp."

"Uh-huh, good idea. Sorry," I said.

This is what I have learned to do when Miss Tibbs lectures me.

1. Agree with whatever she says.

2. Apologize even if I don't know what I did wrong.

When I do that, she usually leaves me alone.

After Miss Tibbs walked away, my friend

Minnie, who was sitting next to me, asked, "Why are you so tired, anyway?"

"Because Little Nicky stole Ricardo, which meant Pearl couldn't sleep—which meant I couldn't sleep, either."

Minnie and I have been friends since we were toddlers, and she knows all about Little Nicky's mischief and Pearl's love for Ricardo.

"Ooooooh," she said, her big brown eyes getting wide. "That's serious."

Cora was sitting across from Minnie, peeling a clementine.

"Why would Little Nicky want Ricardo?" she asked in her squeaky chipmunk voice. "No offense, but . . ."

Cora is so polite that she couldn't bring herself to say what she was thinking. So Minnie said it for her: "Ricardo looks like something the cat dragged in. I mean, actually dragged, with his teeth. Through the mud and dirt and garbage and stuff."

Cora nodded as she peeled a second clementine.

"Who knows why Little Nicky does anything? He's a madman!" I sighed. "And as if that isn't bad enough, I made Ezra cry yesterday. I was trying to cheer him up about Ziggy, but I made him more sad!"

"I'm sure it was an accident!" chirped Cora as she took a third clementine out of her lunch box.

Wish You Were Here

Minnie twirled one of her long black braids and said, "Uh-oh. Looks like someone has a Loco Lunch Box today."

"Loco Lunch Box" is what we call it when Cora's mom throws weird stuff in her lunch box, which she does a lot. Sometimes it's great, but usually a Loco Lunch Box is just terrible. Like this day, when Cora's mom packed three clementines, a tub of cream cheese, and a chunk of cauliflower.

"Want to trade?" Cora asked me, holding out the cauliflower.

Cora is my best, best, best friend. I would do almost anything for her. But I will not take even one bite of cauliflower, not even for Cora. That is where I draw the line.

I despise cauliflower! I detest cauliflower! I deplore cauliflower!

It's exactly like broccoli, only in disguise with

a beautiful name and a pretty white color. Well, you're not tricking this girl, cauliflower! Not for a second!

"No thanks," I told Cora. "But you can have some of my sandwich."

I handed her a piece of my sandwich and also one of the pickles Granny put in a sandwich bag. Minnie gave her half a banana.

"So what are we going to do about Ez?" I asked as we munched. "He's supposed to come over again today."

"It's like they say—laughter is the best medicine," said Minnie. "Unless you have strep throat. Then laughing makes your throat feel like it's on fire."

"Bingo!" I nodded in excitement. "You know, you really should join the Fix-It Friends, Minnie. You're a natural."

"Thanks," said Minnie, "but I'm too busy. I

have to go to Chess Club and fencing and baking class . . . and then of course there's piano. I only have lessons twice a week, but I have to practice every day."

"*Ay caramba!*" I exclaimed. It's Spanish for "Darn it!" Minnie taught it to me. "Don't you ever get bored of playing piano?"

"It's just the opposite!" she replied. "I get bored when I *don't* play piano."

"I think Minnie's right. Ezra needs to laugh," said Cora. "When me and Camille or Bo and Lou are sad, my parents put on funny TV shows. I love the show that has home videos of people and animals making mistakes. Bloopers!"

"Yes! Bloopers are super-duper!" I agreed. "Come over after school today, and we'll watch some with Ezra!"

"Can't," said Minnie. "I have piano."

I groaned a loud groan, and she laughed.

"I can come over," said Cora. "Especially if your grandma can make more pimiento cheese sandwiches. This stuff is scrumptious!"

"Oh, she'll make sandwiches," I promised. "Granny stuffs us full of food."

Chapter 10

Sure enough, as soon as we got home, Granny asked, "Y'all hungry?"

Cora, Ezra, Jude, and I devoured a whole stack of pimiento cheese sandwiches. Then Gramps handed us a big bowl of kettle corn to share, and we all piled onto the couch to watch the bloopers show—even Pearl.

Kettle corn is Gramps's specialty. He makes it exactly the same way he makes regular popcorn, with one difference. Instead of just covering the popcorn with mouthwatering butter, he also covers it with mouthwatering sugar! It's salty *and* sweet.

Kettle corn is so heavenly that it is impossible to be sad when you are eating it. So everyone was in great spirits, even Ezra. What made me extra happy was that Little Nicky wasn't bothering us. He was splashing around in the bathtub with his shark collection.

The first section of the bloopers show was all about people falling down. A bride tripped on her long veil. A toddler toppled over, and his face landed right in a bowl of chocolate ice cream! We were all laughing our heads off.

Then it was time for commercials. My mom cannot stand commercials, but I like them. It's how I learn about new toys I want Mom and Dad to get me.

We watched a funny commercial for car insurance with a talking porcupine and a commercial

for a machine you can use to make your own taffy. I decided I would put it on next year's Christmas list.

Then a commercial popped up that showed a woman lying on a beach, wearing a yellow swimsuit and sun hat. There was a pretty song playing in the background, about three little birds on someone's doorstep. It was bright and cheery and very relaxing. So I was surprised when I heard a gasping sound coming from Ezra.

When I looked over, he was crying.

"What's the matter?" Cora asked.

"This song—" Ezra choked out. "This was Ziggy's favorite. Whenever Mom played it, he would run in circles." He dropped his head into his hands and cried.

I grabbed the remote control and tried to make the volume lower. But I accidentally pressed the "up" button instead of the "down" one, so the volume got louder. The song about the three little birds blasted through the living room. Ezra's crying got louder, too.

"TOO WOWD!" Pearl shouted, covering her ears.

"Turn it off!" yelled Jude.

"I'm TRYING!"

I really was, too. But the batteries in the remote control are old, and sometimes the buttons don't

work so well. So the TV was stuck on the So-Loud-You-Might-Go-Deaf setting.

Finally, Gramps came in and pressed the power button to turn off the TV.

"I'm so sorry, Ezra!" I cried. "I had no idea that was going to happen."

"It's okay," sniffed Ezra. "I'm sorry I'm crying."

Everyone talked at the same time:

"It's all right!"

"Of course you can cry!"

"Don't worry about it!"

"Gary Grotowski said it's weird that I'm so upset," said Ezra. "He said Ziggy was just a guinea pig and I should get over it."

"Gary Grotowski's a blockhead," said Jude. "You know that."

"When I see Gary Grotowski, I'm going to knock him into tomorrow," I promised.

"Sounds like Gary just never had a pet," Gramps piped up. "Because, Ezra, anybody who ever lost a pet has felt just what you feel now. Don't matter if it's a horse or a potbellied pig or a little, bitty field mouse."

Just then, who should barge in but Little Nicky, soaking wet from his bath. He was wearing goggles, a silver swim cap, and absolutely nothing else.

"WHAT IS ALL THIS NOISE?" Little Nicky shouted. "MY SHARKS CAN'T EAT DINNER WITH THIS RACKET!"

Little Nicky looked so funny like that, blazing mad and naked as a mole rat. Naturally, Ezra burst out laughing.

For once in my life, I did not want to clobber Little Nicky. In fact, I wanted to hug him.

Chapter 11

That night, I barely slept. Pearl couldn't fall asleep again, because she missed Ricardo so much. I wished Mom and Dad were home, because they'd know how to get her to sleep and they'd also know how to find Ricardo. But they weren't coming home for another two days. So it was up to me.

"Pearl," I whispered finally, "come sleep with me."

The good news was, she went right to sleep as soon as she climbed into my bed. The bad news is, I did not! How could I sleep with a little body kicking and smacking me all night long?

I never knew this before, but when she sleeps,

Wish You Were Here

Pearl flops around like a fish out of water. She is tiny, but boy, can she pack a punch!

She sleep-kicked me in my ribs. Then she sleep-slapped me in my face. Then she sleep-rolled right on top of me so I couldn't breathe!

I finally drifted off for a while, until a loud snoring sound woke me up. For a second, I thought that an elephant or a rhinoceros had sneaked into my bed. That's how loud the snoring was. But when I opened my eyes, I realized it was just Pearl.

After that, I just lay in bed, thinking. I thought about how much I missed Mom and Dad and how much Pearl missed Ricardo. I thought about how much Ezra missed Ziggy.

I wished there was something we could do to stop Ezra from being sad. I really wanted to call an emergency Fix-It meeting, but it was only 6:13 a.m. And besides, none of our other Fix-It ideas had worked for Ezra. In fact, they'd made everything worse. After all, Ezra was one of the Fix-It Friends' secret weapons; it was hard to fix stuff without him helping.

I thought and I thought. I tapped my fingers on the wall next to my bed because tapping always helps me concentrate. I had to tap them softly so I didn't wake Pearl up, but it worked anyway. At 6:30 a.m., I had a *Eureka!* moment. That's what my dad calls it when he gets a sensational idea.

Wish You Were Here

I carefully rolled Pearl off me and climbed up to the top bunk, where Jude was sleeping. It was too early to bother the whole Fix-It crew, but it's never too early to bother Jude.

I shook him awake.

"No! Please!" he yelped, batting me away with his eyes closed. "Not my brain! Eat my liver! Eat my spleen! Just leave the brain!"

"Shhhh!" I whispered. "It's your sister, not a zombie. Wake up! I know how to fix Ezra, but I need your help."

And after a little more zombie-begging, and a lot of grumbling, good old Jude did help me. By the time we left for school, we were nearly done with the cure for Ezra.

I could not wait to show Principal Powell what we'd done. So when Miss Mabel asked for a volunteer to take the attendance down to the office,

I waved my hand in the air frantically. When I got to the office, I handed Mrs. Rose or Mackenzie the attendance and then I asked her oh-so-politely if I could talk to Principal Powell.

Mrs. Rose or Mackenzie peered at me over the tops of her red eyeglasses: "She's talking to someone, so you'll have to wait. You can read some more about removing warts."

So I did. I learned some interesting stuff, too. Like, to get rid of a wart, you have to freeze it off. I wondered if you really needed a doctor to do that, or if it might happen all on its own, on very cold days. I was thinking that it was probably cold enough right then to freeze warts off, and maybe lots of people would find ice-cold warts rolling around in their socks and gloves and pants. That would be so weird!

My wondering was interrupted when the door

to the principal's office opened. I saw Principal Powell and the back of a boy's head. I recognized that brown buzz cut right away.

Matthew Sawyer!

The thorn in my side!

"So it's agreed, then?" Principal Powell was saying to him. "Someone else will feed the ants for a while."

"But it was an accident!" Matthew Sawyer whined.

"Of course, Matt," said Principal Powell with a smile, "but it is the second time you left the lid open."

Oh brother, I thought, *Matthew Sawyer let the ants in the ant farm loose again!*

Miss Mabel had put him in charge of the ant farm because he loves bugs and he begged her. The trouble is, he is so forgetful! Almost every day, he leaves his homework folder at school. At least once a week, he forgets his winter jacket at school! Practically the whole Lost and Found belongs to him.

A few weeks ago, after he fed the ants, Matthew Sawyer forgot to put the top back on the ant farm. The whole ant army just marched out! For weeks, there were ants everywhere: in our book bins, in the paint jars, and on the whiteboard. When I opened up my math textbook, what do you think crawled out? A whole line of ants! Math is bad enough without an ant attack, too.

And now he'd gone and done it again!

"It could happen to anyone!" grumbled Matthew Sawyer.

"It's all right, Matt." Principal Powell patted his shoulder. "We all make mistakes."

Matthew Sawyer sighed and turned around. Then he saw me and made a grimace.

"What are *you* doing here?" he asked. "Are you supposed to be my punishment?"

I wanted to do a big kung fu kick at him, but I knew Principal Powell was watching so I just smiled sweetly and said, "Oh, Matthew Sawyer, you're *so* silly! A laugh *riot*!"

Then I turned to Principal Powell and told her I had an urgent matter to discuss, and we both walked into her office.

Chapter 12

"So what can I help you with, my dear?" Principal Powell asked.

"It's about Ezra," I said as I sank onto the strawberry cloud couch. "He's sad. Too sad. I haven't even seen him crack his knuckles in days! You know he's always cracking those knuckles when he's excited. And he's not humming music like he always does when he's happy."

Principal Powell nodded.

"The trouble is, he just keeps thinking about Ziggy. Soooooooo—"

I pulled a folded packet of paper out of my pocket.

"I made a list!"

"A list?" asked Principal Powell. She took a sip from her mug. "What kind of list?"

"The title is . . ." I cleared my throat and read out loud. "Every Single Possible Word That Might Remind Ezra of Ziggy, Arranged Alphabetically."

"Wow," said Principal Powell.

"Jude and I only had time to do *A* through *T*." I flipped to the end of the list. "So we got up to *tap dance, tickle torture,* and *toilet.* It's only five pages so far, but we're not done. I think there's a lot we forgot to include. That's why I came. I wanted to see if you had anything we could add. Then, once we've finished it, you can make copies. We'll need enough to give to every kid in the school and also all the teachers. You *do* have a copy machine in this office, don't you?"

Principal Powell didn't say anything. She just sipped from her mug. I listened to the fancy violin music she is always playing. It's nice music, but it would be way better with some words thrown in.

"I love this idea, my dear, but I don't think it will work," she finally said. "In fact, I know it won't."

I was shocked. And so disappointed.

"Why not?"

"Because we couldn't possibly prevent Ezra from thinking about Ziggy. We can't just wipe him out of his memory. And even if we could, we wouldn't want to."

"We wouldn't?" I thought that was *exactly* what we wanted.

"No," said Principal Powell. "Once Ezra feels better, remembering Ziggy will actually be a nice thing for him."

I raised my eyebrows at her. I didn't really believe her, but she was the principal so I couldn't say so.

"What you're trying to do is find a shortcut for Ezra so he can just hop right over the muck of bad feelings and get to the sunny, clear place where he's happy again," said Principal Powell, "but what I'm trying to say is, sometimes you just have to wade through the muck."

"But I just don't want him to get stuck in muck, because . . . yuck!"

Principal Powell laughed. "He won't. It's not fun to be sad, but it's okay. He'll get through."

There was a knock at the door, and Principal Powell called, "Yes, Mrs. Rose?"

Aha! So her name was Mrs. *Rose*! I had to remember that for next time.

"Matthew Sawyer is here to see you again," Mrs. Rose announced.

"All right, thanks," replied Principal Powell. Then she walked me to the door. "You're a wonderful friend, Veronica. I'm so glad Ezra has you in his corner."

My heart swelled up like an enormous balloon.

Then I saw Matthew Sawyer's face and the balloon popped.

"I forgot my coat in there," he explained.

Wish You Were Here

"Matthew Sawyer!" I exclaimed without thinking. "You'd forget your head if it wasn't attached to your shoulders."

"That would be so cool." He grinned. "I'd dress up like the Headless Horseman every Halloween!"

I was speechless. Just speechless.

Chapter 13

That day at recess, it was so cold, my tag gang
didn't play tag. We found a little corner of the
playground where the wind was blocked. Then we
made a tight circle with our knees pulled up to our
chests and our shoulders touching the people next
to us. This creates body warmth and can keep
you alive if you are shipwrecked, even in Alaska. It
is a known fact, no matter what Jude says. I plan
to ask Uncle Eddy about it when he comes back.

We were all trying to decide what to play when
Jude and Ezra passed by. They weren't playing tag,
like they usually do, or reading comic books, or

laughing. They were just walking and kicking a rock.

"Guys!" I called out. "Wanna play Would You Rather?"

Ezra shook his head.

"Twenty Questions?"

More head shaking.

"Name That Song?"

"No thanks," he said as the two of them walked off.

"Wow, things must be bad if Ez doesn't want to play Name That Song!" I said to the others. Then I told them about my great idea to help Ezra and how Principal Powell had rained on my parade.

"She's right," said Minnie. She was wearing an enormous pair of fuzzy white earmuffs. "Remember my cousin Valentina, who used to live next door to me? My best friend? Remember when she moved to Puerto Rico last year? I cried so much! I used six boxes of tissues in one week! I thought I'd never stop feeling so bad. But, finally, I did."

"If my cousin moved to Puerto Rico, I'd be over-joyed," I chimed in. "But it would be even better if he moved to Siberia."

Everyone laughed.

"That's what happened to me when my brother went to college," said my friend J.J. His face was almost hidden by a huge orange scarf wrapped around his neck. "I still miss him, but it's just not a big deal anymore. I got used to it."

"So we're just supposed to sit back and wait?"

"Pretty much," said J.J.

Then quiet Noah piped up. He hardly ever talks, so when he speaks, we all listen. "My dad always says, 'Time heals all wounds.'"

"Well, not *all* wounds," Minnie said. "Time

won't heal an anaconda bite. You need an antidote for that."

"But I can't stand just waiting!" I said. "I mean, I'm the president of the Fix-It Friends, for crying out loud—"

"Technically, you're not," Cora interrupted. But I couldn't reply, because I was on a roll.

"We can't just twiddle our thumbs and do nothing!"

The Fix-It Friends

"Well, why don't we ask him what *he* wants?" squeaked Cora.

Good old sensible Cora.

"It's so simple, it just might work!" I exclaimed.

I ripped off a blank piece of paper from the big list of things never to say to Ezra. Then we all helped write this note:

Dear Ezra,

What can we do to make you feel better?

1. Take you to Disneyland?

2. Buy you a new computer?

3. Take you to the zoo to visit those weird spiders you like?

4. Give you a makeover?

5. Finish making *Shimmy Strikes Back*?

6. Open up a nacho stand in the lobby of the Monroe?

7. Give you a coconut you can attack with a screwdriver?

8. Fill in the blank: _____

Sincerely,

The Fix-It Friends

When we finished, I tried to find Ezra to give it to him, but he must have gone to the bathroom or his mom's office. I found Jude, though, crossing out stuff on his Lost and Found list.

"Lots of stuff was claimed," he said oh-so-happily. "Matthew Sawyer's stepdad came and collected seven gloves, three hats, one lunch box, and a sneaker."

"A *sneaker*?" I asked. I shook my head in disbelief.

"Can you give this to Ezra?" I asked Jude, handing him the note.

Jude read the note and frowned. He crossed out items one, two, and six.

"No Disneyland, computer, or nacho stand," he said. "Not realistic. The rest are okay."

I rolled my eyes. It drives me so crazy when he acts like a grown-up. I mean, aren't there *enough* grown-ups in the world already? We don't need another one who is really just a kid!

Chapter 14

That afternoon, when Granny and Pearl came to pick us up from school, Pearl had a humongous smile on her face.

There, on her lap, peeking out from under her blue fleece blanket, was a little black, furry face.

"Ricardo?"

"Gwanny found him!" Pearl exclaimed.

I looked more closely at Ricardo's face.

"He looks different," I said. "He's got his whiskers back."

"Yeah, and he looks really clean," agreed Jude. "Did you wash him?"

"Goodness gracious, I've never seen children so troubled to see something clean and fixed up. Don't you worry about it, sugars."

I smiled. Granny was right. The important thing was, Ricardo was found. Now Pearl could be happy again. And I could get a good night's sleep.

Granny brought me to gymnastics class, where I almost did a back walkover all by myself! I called into the waiting area for Jude to watch, but he could not tear his eyes away from the book he was reading, *The Quest of Queen Kong.*

As soon as we got home, I walked into my room. I'd had a long day, and all I wanted to do was flop onto my bed and read *How to Talk So Dogs Will Listen.*

But I couldn't flop onto my bed. Because someone was already on it!

Wish You Were Here

No, it was not Goldilocks. If only it were! I always had a feeling the two of us would get along.

It was Little Nicky!

With his shoes on!

And his feet on my pillow!

He was reading a book about—what else?—sharks. Except that I could tell he wasn't really reading it, just making up the words.

"THIS KIND OF SHARK IS CALLED THE MONKEY-HEAD PURPLE-NOSE SHARK. IT CAN TRAVEL FOUR MILLION MILES AN HOUR. IT EATS GRIZZLY BEARS FOR BREAK-FAST AND IT SPEAKS FRENCH."

Granny, Pearl, Jude, and I stood in the door-way, watching him.

I gave a look to Jude that said, *He's bonkers!* And Jude gave me a look back that said, *Didn't you already know that?* And I gave *him* a look back that said, *Yeah, but not quite how much!*

The great thing about brothers is, you can say all this stuff without any words.

Pearl looked scared. She clutched Ricardo very tight and tugged on Granny's hand.

"Gwanny, bath time," said Pearl, pulling Granny out of the doorway.

Little Nicky kept pretend-reading: "THIS NEXT SHARK RIGHT HERE IS CALLED THE PLAGOBLAGOYAYA SHARK. IT LIVES IN ANTARCTICA AND IS SANTA'S PERSONAL SHARK. HE LIKES CHILDREN AND HE MAKES A GOOD PET."

I was furious.

"Can you *please* get your feet off my pillow?"

But instead of getting off my bed, or taking off

his shoes, Little Nicky just kicked my pillow off the bed. Then he kept on reading.

"NOW WE COME TO THE BEST SHARK IN THE UNIVERSE. IT IS CALLED THE NICH-OLAS SHARK. IT IS KNOWN FOR BEING THE SMARTEST SHARK IN THE OCEAN. WHEN HUMANS SEE IT, THEY RUN SCREAMING. SOMETIMES THEY ARE SO SCARED, THEY EVEN PEE THEIR PANTS."

Jude couldn't take any more: "Sorry, Little Nicky, but I need to do my homework in this room. Can you find somewhere else to go?"

"WELL, I'M DOING MY HOMEWORK, TOO," Little Nicky insisted. "BUT I NEED TO WEAR YOUR GLASSES TO DO IT. GIVE 'EM TO ME."

I could see that Jude wanted to rip that book out of Little Nicky's hands and shred it into a thousand pieces, then burn those pieces in a bonfire.

But Jude is pretty good at keeping his temper. He took a deep breath and said, "Sorry, Little Nicky, but these glasses are not a toy. I need them to see."

"SO DO I." Little Nicky pouted.

Jude bit his lip to keep from shouting. "I guess I'll take my shower before I do my homework tonight. Maybe it'll be relaxing." Then Jude slipped

off his tortoiseshell glasses and handed them to me.

He whispered, "I'll be in Mom and Dad's bathroom. Guard these with your life."

"AND NOW FOR THE SLOWEST SHARK IN THE WORLD. IT IS CALLED THE VERONI-CACA SHARK AND IT HAS YELLOW HAIR AND BLUE EYES. IT IS SLOW. IT HAS NO TEETH. IT IS THE WORST."

"Little Nicky!" I cried. "Are you talking about ME?"

He looked up at me oh-so-innocently. "I'M JUST TALKING ABOUT THE SHARK THAT HAS THE SAME NAME AS YOU."

"Veroni-caca is not my name and you know it!"

"OKAY, VERONI-CACA!" he shouted. Then he exploded into the biggest, meanest laughing fit you ever heard. He was laughing so hard, he was kicking all the sheets and stuffed animals on my bed, with his dumb shoes still on!

I marched right over to where he was lying. I held my finger up to his face, like I meant business.

"You better cut that out right now!"

But he did not cut it out. In fact, he laughed even louder.

I was about to grab him by his collar and throw him off my bed. But before I could do anything,

I heard a bloodcurdling scream coming from the bathroom downstairs. I dropped everything, including Jude's glasses, and ran downstairs to help.

At first, nothing looked wrong. Pearl was sitting in the tub and Granny was standing next to her, trying to calm her down. Then I looked closely at the bathwater. It wasn't clear the way water should be. It was gray. It looked like the gross puddles near the sewers when it rains.

I didn't know what to think. Then a terrible idea popped into my mind. Our house was haunted! It was the only possible explanation.

"Begone, ye ghosts!" I yelled. "BEGONE!!"

"Oh, for heaven's sake, there are no ghosts," cried Granny. Then she turned to Pearl and said, "Sugar, I told you Ricardo couldn't go in the bath!"

That's when I saw that Ricardo was lying at the bottom of the tub, and Pearl was kicking him

away. Except it didn't quite look like Ricardo. Because *this* rat wasn't black. This rat was white with gray splotches.

"It's not Wicawdo!" Pearl wailed.

Granny lifted Pearl out of the dirty water, wrapped her in a fluffy towel, and gave her a big hug.

"Granny and Gramps just wanted to make you happy. So we went to the store where your mama got Ricardo, to get a new one. But they only had the kind with white fur. So we thought, 'Heck, that's nothing a little spot of black dye can't fix.'"

I gasped. "You mean, this Ricardo is an impostor?"

"I suppose so," Granny said.

"I want MY Wicawdo!" Pearl sobbed, burying her head in Granny's shoulder.

Wish You Were Here

Before I could say anything, I heard another scream. This one was coming from my other sibling.

"LITTLE NICKY, you have gone TOO FAR!"

"BUT IT WAS AN ACCIDENT!"

I ran in and saw Little Nicky holding Jude's glasses.

Well, half of Jude's glasses. The other half was lying on my bed.

Jude was wearing his bathrobe. His face was flaming red.

"And YOU!" yelled Jude, spinning to face me. "I told you to guard them with your life! I knew I couldn't trust you!"

I was aghast!

"I am aghast!" I exclaimed.

I know it seems like I made that word up, but I did not. It means "horrified." Jude taught it to me.

"*I'm* the one who's aghast!" yelled Jude. "*You* are a pest! That's what you are! A pest!"

Then Jude grabbed both halves of his glasses and stormed out of the room. I felt so furious and sad and confused. All of a sudden, I missed Mom and Dad so much, I couldn't stand it.

I dashed to the phone and dialed Mom's number, but she didn't pick up. So I left a really long message.

Wish You Were Here

"Mom, help! Everything is a disaster. Pearl lost Ricardo, and we thought we found him, but it turns out the new Ricardo is an impostor! And Little Nicky broke Jude's glasses, and now he's probably blinded for life! And worst of all, Ziggy died and Ezra's miserable. We need you! Please fly home ASAP. If no planes are available, you may have to take a private jet. I'm sure there are plenty of private jets in California because that's where the movie stars live. So, please, hurry home! And, if you can, try to stop at Disneyland on the way and get me a pair of Mickey Mouse ears, because I have always wanted those."

After I hung up, I was so sad and tired that I went to bed. It was so early, I didn't even have any dinner or anything, but I didn't care. I was just ready for the day to be over.

Chapter 15

The next morning at breakfast, Jude was wearing his glasses again. Except now, they had a big lump of silver duct tape in the middle, over his nose.

"Hey, cool duct tape!" I chirped. "Remember when I used to think the word was *duck tape*, and I asked Dad why so many poor ducks had to lose their lives to make that tape?"

But I could not sweet-talk him. Jude just glared at me as he ate his yogurt.

"Morning, sunshine," said Gramps, who was frying up sausage links at the stove. "Your mama

called last night. We told her you were out like a light, and she said she'd try back today."

"I'll just call her now," I said.

"Pumpkin, it's only four in the morning in California." Gramps laughed. "You call your mama at this hour, and she'll be crankier than a coyote with a bee sting."

I sighed. It felt like I'd never get to talk to my parents again.

Later that day, at recess, Ezra did something surprising. He called an immediate Fix-It Friends meeting, right there on the spot. Jude refused to stand next to me or even look in my direction.

"I thought you didn't want to talk about your . . . umm, your trouble," I said to him.

"I didn't," he said, "but I got your note and it got me thinking. I know what will help."

He cracked his knuckles. That sound made me so happy!

"A memorial for Ziggy," he said. "That's what I want."

"Ez." Jude smiled. "That's perfect."

"My mom says we can do it this weekend, at my apartment," he said.

"Don't worry, Ezra. We'll take care of everything!" Cora promised him.

After school, I went to Cora's house to plan

the memorial. I needed a break from mean Little Nicky and sad Pearl and angry Jude.

Cora and I had a great brainstorming session, and by the time Gramps picked me up, we had planned almost everything. We had a few special surprises up our sleeve.

When I got home, Jude was sitting at his desk doing his homework. He had a different pair of glasses on.

"Hey, where'd you get those?"

I was ready for the silent treatment again, but he didn't seem so angry anymore. I guess time really does heal all wounds.

"This is my old pair, from last year," Jude replied. "Mom told Granny where to find them."

I swallowed hard. "Mom called? I missed her again?"

Jude nodded. I ran into the living room and

dialed Mom's number, but it went right to voice mail. I hung up and tried not to cry.

"Oh, sugar, their phones are off. They're already on the plane," Granny said as she put her arm around my shoulder. "They'll be home real late tonight. When you wake up, they'll be here!"

I nodded.

"Want to help me fix dessert?"

Because Granny and Gramps live in Texas,

sometimes they use different words than I do. Like they say *Putt-Putt* instead of *mini golf* and *supper* instead of *dinner* and *fix* instead of *cook*. So, if the Fix-It Friends lived in Texas, our job might be to make food for people!

Granny smiled. "I was gonna fix coconut cream pie."

"Can we put whipped cream on top?"

"You can't have pie without whipped cream," answered Granny.

My thoughts exactly.

Chapter 16

When the pie was done, I brought a slice to Pearl. She was in her bedroom, looking at our old photo album. She was staring at a photo of herself on her second birthday, pulling Ricardo out of wrapping paper.

"Here you go," I said, handing her the pie. "This'll make you feel better."

But when I handed the plate to her, the fork slid off and clattered to the floor.

It slid under her bookshelf, so I had to stick my hand under there to grab it. That's when I felt something furry.

Wish You Were Here

I pulled at it, but it was wedged in tight. So I stuck both hands under the shelf and tugged and tugged until—

Pop! The furry thing came loose and went flying out of my hands across the room, right onto Pearl's lap.

"Wicawdo!" she cried.

I scrambled over to her and inspected the stuffed animal on her lap. I wanted to make sure it was the real deal.

1. Dirty black fur? Check!

2. No whiskers at all? Check!

3. Tail stuck on with duct tape? Check!

"It *is* Ricardo!" I exclaimed. "Hallelujah!"

"Hawawuwa!" Pearl repeated.

She clutched Ricardo to her chest and squeezed him with all her might.

"Another happy customer," I said, crossing my

arms in front of my chest. I was terrifically proud that I'd solved her problem all on my own, without the other Fix-Its.

"Little Nicky must have hid Ricardo under there." I gritted my teeth. "When I get my hands on him . . ."

Pearl's eyes grew enormously big. Then she shook her head.

"I did it," she said.

"You stuffed Ricardo under the bookshelf?"

"To make him safe. Fwom Nicky." She nodded. "But I fowgot."

I shook my head in disbelief. "I hate to say this, but I think we owe someone an apology."

Little Nicky was not very nice about the whole thing. Big surprise.

"I TOLD YOU I DIDN'T TAKE THAT RAT." Little Nicky crossed his arms and glared at me.

"I know, and I'm sorry I didn't believe you."

I thought my apology would put him in a good mood, but it did not. He just got madder and madder. He stood up and started waving his arms as he shouted.

"AND I DIDN'T MEAN TO BREAK THOSE GLASSES."

"I know, and I'm sorry we yelled at you."

Little Nicky was getting so mad that he was stomping his feet.

"AND I HATE SLEEPING ON PINK SHEETS AND YOUR TOILET IS TOO LOUD AND THE HOT CHOCOLATE YOU GOT ISN'T SWEET ENOUGH."

I didn't know what to say to that.

"AND I HATE STUPID YOGA AND I WANT TO GO ON MY DAD'S SHIP BUT THEY DON'T LET KIDS AND—AND—AND I MISS MAMA AND DAAAAAAADDY!"

Then Little Nicky plopped down on the floor and started to cry. He cried just as loud as he talked.

I stood there, shocked. I would never have guessed that Little Nicky was missing his parents! Thankfully, Pearl knew just what to do. She

walked over to him and handed him Ricardo to squeeze. Then she told Granny that Little Nicky needed a piece of pie. That girl's a Fix-It Friend in the making!

Between the rat and the pie and Pearl being nice, Little Nicky cheered up right quick, as Granny would say. Then both he and Pearl fell asleep with no problems. Which meant I did, too.

Chapter 17

"Rise and shine, sleepyhead."

At first, I thought it was the voice of the Yorkshire terrier who was flying the helicopter in my dream. But then I heard the voice again, and it sounded familiar. It was not the voice of a Yorkie pilot! It was the voice of my mother!

I squinted open one eye and there she was—her hazel eyes, her blond hair, her dangly earrings—sitting right on my bed!

"MOM!" I shouted as I threw my arms around her waist.

"What a welcome! We should go on vacation

more often" came Dad's voice. He was there, too, standing right next to Mom. I clambered out of bed and jumped into his bear hug.

"Mom? Dad?" came Jude's voice from the top bunk. In a flash, he'd scrambled down the ladder and was hugging them, too.

The racket woke Pearl. She crawled off the air mattress in the corner, holding Ricardo, and clamped her arms tight around Dad's leg.

"I tried to call you a bunch of times," Mom said. "Is everything okay?"

"Of course!" I exclaimed. "Why wouldn't it be?"

"Well, you left us a pretty desperate message," said Dad.

"If I recall correctly, the words *disaster* and *ASAP* and *get on a private jet* were used," Mom added.

"Oh, *that*." I smiled. "That was the day before yesterday."

"We handled it," Jude said.

Gramps made eggs sunny-side up while we told Mom and Dad all about Ricardo and fake Ricardo and Ezra and Ziggy and everything.

"Want to come to Ziggy's memorial?" I asked Mom, Dad, Granny, and Gramps. "It's tomorrow."

"It would be an honor," said Mom.

Gramps offered to bring kettle corn, and Granny said she'd fix a coconut cream pie.

Dad agreed to help Jude with a very special project he was working on for the memorial. Jude needed a guy with a drill, and Dad was just the guy.

The next morning, we all headed over to the Monroe, which is where Ezra lives. My whole family came, even Little Nicky and Pearl. Cora's whole family came, too, including her five-year-old twin brothers, Bo and Lou. Little Nicky followed them around everywhere, doing exactly what they did. You could tell he thought they were almost as great as hammerhead sharks.

Minnie and her moms came, with a cheesecake that Minnie had made herself in baking class. Noah came with his cool teenage babysitter, Ivy. A whole bunch of Ezra's neighbors from the Monroe came, even grumpy Mr. Luntzgarten, who lives on the fourth floor and hates children.

Speaking of grumpy people, Mrs. Rose was there, too. She asked me how I was doing with my wart problem. She had a twinkle in her eye.

Even Miss Tibbs came. It gave me the heebie-jeebies to see her somewhere outside of the school building. It was like seeing a tiger out of the zoo.

"I brought a fruitcake," she said, putting something that looked like a big heavy brick on the table full of food.

Of course Miss Tibbs brought a fruitcake. It's the one thing with the word *cake* in it that I would never eat.

"There's nothing like a good fruitcake. It's *reliable*," said Mr. Luntzgarten, who was filling his plate. "You wouldn't believe the cockamamy dishes people bring nowadays."

"I would believe it because I've seen it with my own eyes," said Miss Tibbs. She was getting excited and gesturing with her hands. "Quinoa! Quiche! Quince jam! It's a disgrace!"

That's when the most wonderful idea popped up in my brain!

"Mr. Luntzgarten, this is Miss Tibbs," I said. "Miss Tibbs, this is Mr. Luntzgarten."

"Call me Seymour," he said, sticking out his hairy hand.

She shook his hand, and her cheeks turned a little red.

"I'm Eleanor," she replied.

ELEANOR???? I thought.

In a million years, I never thought I'd find out Miss Tibbs's first name. Or that it would be Eleanor.

I walked away from the two of them, and my heart was racing with excitement. It was love at first sight! They'd probably get married, and I'd finally get to be a flower girl! I'd probably have to wear a black dress and sprinkle black flower petals because Miss Tibbs would definitely wear a black wedding gown, because she always wears black. But that would be okay with me.

A few minutes later, when it seemed like everyone had arrived at the memorial, Jude handed out programs he made.

The Fix-It Friends

Remembering Ziggy

1. Opening remarks by Mary Powell
2. Guests can share a story about Ziggy
3. Musical performance by Veronica Laverne Conti
4. Speech by Ezra Ray Powell
5. Unveiling of the Ziggy Memorial Statue by Jude B. Conti

Principal Powell welcomed everyone, and then people shared Ziggy stories. Most of the stories were funny. At first I wasn't sure if it was okay to laugh. After all, Ziggy was dead. But when I looked

over at Ezra and Principal Powell, they were laughing, so I figured it was all right.

Jude told a story about when he lost his favorite mechanical pencil and searched Ezra's whole apartment for it.

"It was a very rare kind of pencil. It had a non-slip grip, durable lead, and a perfect point—"

I cleared my throat, which is the international signal for *You're boring everyone to tears. Get to the point!*

"So anyway, I was standing in the kitchen, and I heard Ziggy squeaking like crazy. I walked over, and I saw that my pencil was lying on the floor, next to his cage."

He shook his head in amazement. "He knew! He just knew."

Dad made a little speech, too.

"I'm the super in this building, so I've met almost all the pets that live here. Most of them give me trouble," said Dad. "The stories I could tell you! Bearded dragons are the worst because their crickets are always getting loose. But Ziggy never gave me any problems. No noise complaints. No odor issues. He was a dream pet."

Then it was Mom's turn. "Over the years, we've had the pleasure of pet-sitting for Ziggy when the Powells went away. I always enjoyed the time Ziggy spent with us. I know we all miss him dearly. But, as the great poet Alfred, Lord Tennyson said, ''Tis better to have loved and lost than never to have loved at all.'"

Good old Mom. She has a famous quote for every occasion.

Wish You Were Here

After the stories, it was time for my musical performance. Cora had found a karaoke version of the song about the three birds, and she played it on her mom's phone. I sang along on the microphone I got for Christmas.

I thought of Ziggy as I sang. It's a really nice song because it says over and over, "Every little thing is gonna be all right." As I sang it, I started to really believe it.

When I was done, everyone clapped and I took a little bow. Then Ezra walked to the front of the room. He took a deep breath and started to speak. Even though it's usually hard to understand what Ezra says because he talks so fast, on this day, his voice was slow and calm.

"That was Ziggy's favorite song. I love it, too. It just makes you feel good. Like, even on the days when you're sad and it feels like you're frozen from the tips of your toes to the tips of your fingers. Even on those days, if you listen to the song, a tiny piece of you starts to feel warm, like the sun is shining on you and melting the ice away. And the more you listen, the more melts away, and the better you feel.

"Ziggy did the same thing for me. If I ever had a terrible day at school, I would take Ziggy out of his cage. We'd play fetch or I'd feed him hay or just pet him, and I'd start to feel a little better. Things were never as bad as they seemed."

Ezra wiped a bunch of tears away then, but I didn't hand him a tissue because I needed them for my own face.

"Ziggy, you were a great friend. I'll miss you a lot. But you'll always be with me, in my heart."

Then Ezra sat down and his mom gave his shoulder a squeeze.

Wish You Were Here

After that, it was time for Jude to unveil the special gift he had made. He carried a shoe box to the front of the room and lifted out a small clay statue that looked just like Ziggy. There was a wooden base under the statue, and the sign on the base said:

In loving memory of
Ziggy Stardust Powell
Pet, Dreamer, Friend

By the time the memorial was over, there was not a single tissue left in the box.

Chapter 18

The next day was Sunday, the day Gramps and Granny had to leave. Little Nicky, too.

I could not wait for Pearl to move back into her own room. I was tired of guarding all my special stuff from Little Nicky and tired of hearing facts about sharks. I was counting down the days until Sunday.

But when Sunday came, I felt sorry they were leaving.

"I'll miss you, sugar," Granny said to me. "But we'll see you real soon."

"And remember, if you get a hankering for

kettle corn, your mama knows my secret recipe," said Gramps with a wink. "Just don't let her skimp on the sugar."

"I won't," I said, giving him a huge squeeze.

"Say thank you to your cousins for being such good hosts, Little Nicky," Granny instructed.

"THANK YOU," Little Nicky said as he walked to the door, with his enormous backpack on his little back. But when he got to the door, he paused. Then he unzipped his backpack and pulled out one of his plastic sharks. He walked over to Pearl and handed it to her.

"YOU DON'T HAVE ANY SHARKS IN THIS PLACE," he said. "YOU CAN HAVE THIS ONE IF YOU WANT. IT'S A HAMMERHEAD BABY. I NAMED IT RALPH BUT YOU CAN CHANGE THE NAME."

"Thank you," said Pearl with a smile.

"JUST DON'T PUT IT NEAR A GREAT WHITE," said Little Nicky very seriously. "THEY DON'T GET ALONG."

Pearl nodded.

"OKAY BYE," said Little Nicky. And then all three of them were gone.

With Little Nicky gone, things in our house were very calm. Almost too calm. Pretty boring, in fact. So, two weeks later, on another freezing-cold Sunday, Cora and I were complaining to Dad about how there was nothing to do. I had put on my curly red wig and tried to use cuteness mind control on Dad so he'd let us play with his staple gun, but it didn't work. Cora was just about to try talking to him when the phone rang.

Jude picked up and we heard him say, "Oh, hi!" and then "Uh-huh. . . . Really? Yeah, Ronny and

Cora are here. . . . Right now? . . . I don't know. I'll ask my dad."

Then he said, "Dad? Can we all go over to Ezra's house? He says he's got a surprise to show us."

Cora and I shrieked so loudly that it almost broke Dad's eardrums. So he said, "Sure."

The whole way over, I tried to guess what the surprise was.

"He's taking us to Disneyland! That would be great! I never did get those Mickey Mouse ears I wanted."

Jude shook his head.

"Maybe it's a karaoke machine. Ezra does love music. Or a balance beam? Oh! Oh! I know what it is! It's a ROBOT!" I shrieked. "Yes! That has to be it! Ezra has always wanted a robot! Remember when he tried to make one and—"

I was annoying Dad so much that he stopped

in a deli on the way and bought me an enormous jawbreaker just to make me stop talking. Sometimes being a chatterbox has advantages.

When we got to Ezra's apartment, he told us to sit on the couch and close our eyes. A minute later, I felt something on my lap. It was really warm. And soft. And it was purring.

I opened my eyes and saw the fluffiest, tiniest, sweetest kitten you have ever seen. It was completely black with eyes that were yellow and twinkly. I was too happy to gasp. I just stared in amazement at the little creature.

"Meet Sergeant Pepper," said Ezra, who was smiling from ear to ear. "We call him Pep for short."

"He's wonderful," Cora cooed.

"Absolutely perfect," I whispered.

"I think we just found the star for our next movie," said Jude.

Wish You Were Here

"I was thinking the same thing," agreed Ezra.

"He sure is a cutie," said Dad, scratching behind Pep's ears. "Makes me really wish I wasn't allergic."

"He's actually hypoallergenic," Ezra said.

"Is that true?" asked Dad. "Huh. Something to think about."

My heart skipped a beat.

Could it be? Dare I dream?

I knew just what to put on my next Christmas list!

Take the Fix-It Friends Pledge!

I, (say your full name), do solemnly vow to help kids with their problems. I promise to be kind with my words and actions. I will try to help very annoying brothers even though they probably won't ever need help because they're soooooo perfect. Cross my heart, hope to cry, eat a gross old garbage fly.

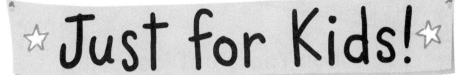

What's in Your Grieving Toolbox?

FIX-IT TOOLBOX

Talk about your feelings.

Keep doing the stuff you love.

Know that it's not your fault.

Don't be scared of sadness.

Find a way to say good-bye.

When Your Pet Dies . . .

All pets—big or small; young or old; furry, feathered, or scaly—are part of the family. When they die, you might feel sad or angry or confused or guilty. You might feel all these things, or you might not feel much of anything at all. However you feel, it's totally okay. It's all a part of grieving and of getting used to life without them.

How did you feel?

"I felt empty. I felt like I wanted to be alone."

—Henry G., age eleven, owner of Lief the cat

"I felt really sad, and I didn't want to go to school, because I was afraid that I would start crying in the middle of class."

—Willa, age eight, owner of Fez the cat

"I was like, what am I going to do? I was super scared that my two gerbils were going to die, too. It was really hard for me to go to sleep. I actually had nightmares."

—**Finley, age eight, owner of Murray the cat**

What helps?

"I talked to people about Thai, and I told them what I felt. Sharing my emotions helped take the weight off of my shoulders."

—**Edie, age eleven, owner of Thai the cat**

"I did schoolwork, and it took my mind off of it."

—**Jorja, age ten, owner of Chester the dog**

"We had a funeral service in the park. That helped a little bit; it made me feel like he was a part of my family and that he really mattered."

—**Claire, age nine, owner of Arnie the rat**

How do you feel now?

"Now when it comes up, I kind of feel sad but for only a second or two, and then I just go back to what I was doing."

—Henry H., age eleven, owner of Arnie the rat

"I really loved Mr. Black and Mr. White, but I had to say good-bye. Their spirit will always be in my heart, forever."

—Stella, age eight, owner of Mr. Black and Mr. White, two fish

What to Do When Your Pet Dies

No one likes feeling upset. We all wish sometimes that we could hit fast-forward on the sad feelings and get straight to the part where we're laughing again. We can't, of course. Feeling bad when a pet dies is as natural as feeling great when you first bring the pet home.

Even though there's no magic cure for your sadness, there are plenty of things you can do that'll make you feel a whole lot better.

1. When you're ready, talk about how you feel.

You may not want to talk about your pet's death right away, and that's totally fine. When you're ready, though, you should share your feelings with someone you trust. Sadness works kind of like a certain annoying little cousin—if you completely ignore it, it'll just keep popping up and giving you trouble. But if you face the feeling by talking about it, it won't bother you so much. You'll actually feel a lot better.

2. Keep doing the stuff you love.

You may not be in the mood for soccer practice or school or a friend's birthday party, and you may be nervous about suddenly getting sad in the middle of it all. But the best way to feel like yourself again is to keep doing all the stuff you normally do. If you get sad, no big deal. Just take a little break until you're ready to jump back in.

3. Know that it's not your fault.

Sometimes people can feel guilty or responsible when a pet dies, like maybe if they'd done something differently, the pet might still be alive. But your pet didn't die because of anything you did or didn't do; it's just something that happens.

4. Don't be scared of sadness.

Feeling sad isn't fun, but it's not dangerous and it's nothing to be scared of. You'll be okay. Know why? Feelings don't last forever. In fact, they change pretty darn fast. Most people feel delighted, disappointed, angry, thankful, jealous—all before lunchtime. It's part of what keeps life interesting.

5. Say good-bye.

Find a way to celebrate your pet's life, either by yourself or with others. Maybe you want to hold a funeral or a memorial service; maybe you want to place a plaque in the backyard or hang up a photo in your living room. The important thing is to do something special that gives you the chance to remember the good times with your pet, and to say good-bye.

Want more tips or fixes for other problems? Just want to check out some Fix-It Friends games and activities? Go to fixitfriendsbooks.com!

Resources for Parents

If your child is grieving the loss of a pet, these resources might help.

Books for Kids

The Day Tiger Rose Said Goodbye by Jane Yolen, Random House, 2011

Dog Heaven by Cynthia Rylant, Blue Sky Press, 1995

The Invisible String by Patrice Karst, Devorss & Co., 2000

Saying Goodbye to Lulu by Corinne Demas, Little, Brown Books, 2009

The Tenth Good Thing About Barney by Judith Viorst, Atheneum Books, 1987

Books for Parents

The Loss of a Pet: A Guide to Coping with the Grieving Process When a Pet Dies, 4th edition by Wallace Sife, PhD, Howell Book House, 2014

Websites

The American Humane Association

Pet Loss Resources

americanhumane.org/fact-sheet/pet-loss-grief/

The Association for Pet Loss and Bereavement

www.aplb.org

The National Child Traumatic Stress Network

www.nctsn.org

Don't miss the next adventure of

The Fix-It Friends

Eyes on the Prize!

About the Author

Nicole C. Kear grew up in New York City, where she still lives with her husband, three firecracker kids, and a ridiculously fluffy hamster. She's written lots of essays and a memoir, *Now I See You*, for grown-ups, and she's thrilled to be writing for kids, who make her think hard and laugh harder. She has a bunch of fancy, boring diplomas and one red clown nose from circus school. Seriously.

nicolekear.com

31901062409489